PALEO SHARKS

Survival of the Strangest

WRITTEN AND ILLUSTRATED BY TIMOTHY J. BRADLEY

chronicle books · san francisco

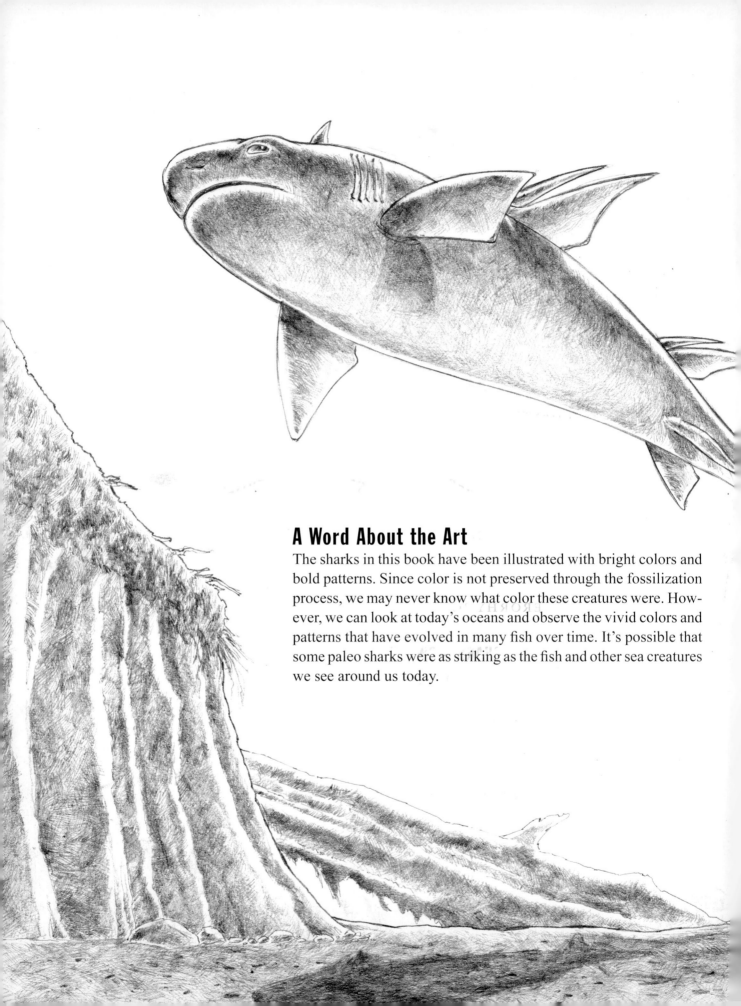

A Word About the Art

The sharks in this book have been illustrated with bright colors and bold patterns. Since color is not preserved through the fossilization process, we may never know what color these creatures were. However, we can look at today's oceans and observe the vivid colors and patterns that have evolved in many fish over time. It's possible that some paleo sharks were as striking as the fish and other sea creatures we see around us today.

CONTENTS

Timeline

TO HELP ORGANIZE THE PAST, scientists divide it into chunks of time. The largest of these chunks is called an eon. Eons are broken down into eras. The sharks in this book lived during three different eras: the Paleozoic era, the Mesozoic era, and the Cenozoic era.

As far as scientists know, animals first appeared on Earth during the Paleozoic era. The middle part of this era, from about 408 to 360 million years ago is known as the Age of Fishes. Many of the sharks in this book appeared during that time. The dinosaurs appeared during the Mesozoic era, which is also known as the Age of Reptiles. We are living in the most recent part of the Cenozoic era, known as the Age of Mammals.

What marks the end of an era? An extinction event is a huge catastrophe—like a meteor strike or a drastic change in Earth's climate—that wipes out large numbers of plants and animals. An extinction event occurred about 65 million years ago, marking the end of the Mesozoic era. At that time, dinosaurs (except for birds), marine reptiles, and the flying pterosaurs became extinct. The extinction event at the end of the Paleozoic era killed off almost all life on this planet.

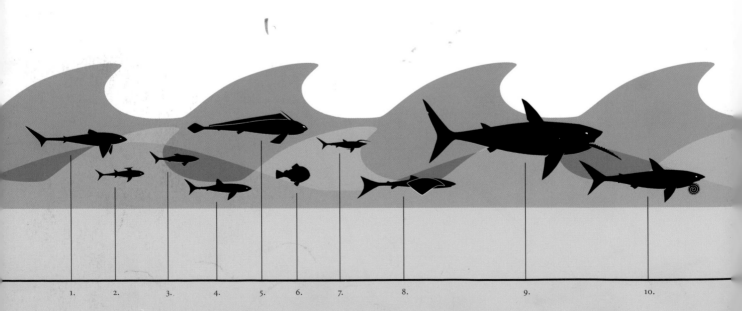

| 1. | 2. | 3. | 4. | 5. | 6. | 7. | 8. | 9. | 10. |

PALEOZOIC ERA

about 543 to 290 million years ago

THESE NUMBERS WILL TELL YOU WHICH SHARK IS WHICH ON THE TIMELINE BELOW.

1. CLADOSELACHE *375 million years ago*
2. STETHACANTHUS *375 million years ago*
3. DOLIODUS *360 million years ago*
4. PUCAPAMPELLA *360 million years ago*
5. ORTHACANTHUS *360 million years ago*
6. BELANTSEA *350 million years ago*
7. FALCATUS *320 million years ago*
8. PROMEXYELE *300 million years ago*
9. EDESTUS *300 million years ago*
10. HELICOPRION *250 million years ago*

11. HYBODUS *180 million years ago*
12. PALAEOSPINAX *180 million years ago*
13. ISCHYODUS *160 million years ago*
14. SPATHOBATHIS *150 million years ago*
15. PALAEOCARCHARIAS *150 million years ago*
16. PROTOSPINAX *150 million years ago*
17. SCLERORHYNCHUS *80 million years ago*

18. CARCHARODON MEGALODON *25 million years ago*

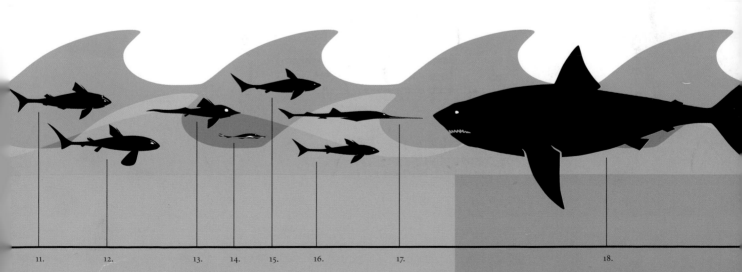

11.　　12.　　　13.　14.　15.　16.　　　17.　　　　　　　　　18.

MESOZOIC ERA
about 250 to 141 million years ago

CENOZOIC ERA
about 65 million years ago to present

What Is a Shark?

IMAGINE: YOU ARE SWIMMING in the ocean, not too far out from shore, when you see it—a large fin slicing through the water.

What is your first reaction? If you are afraid, you are not alone. Many people think that sharks are nothing more than machine-like killers. The truth is, sharks are complex and efficient predators that occupy an important place in the world's oceans. Some sharks feed on sick and injured sea creatures. Some are bottom-dwellers and munch on shellfish.

Scientifically speaking, sharks are chondrichthyans (kon-DRIK-thee-ans), or fish with skeletons made of cartilage (KART-il-uj). Cartilage is something like bone but lighter and more flexible. About 450 million years ago, in the Paleozoic era, there were two major groups of chondrichthyans. One group, the elasmobranchs (ee-LAZ-moe-branks), evolved over millions of years into the sharks and rays in our oceans today. All of the fish mentioned in this book, except *Pucapampella, Belantsea, Promexyele,* and *Ischyodus,* are elasmobranchs. The other group of chondrichthyans, called holocephalians (hol-oh-seff-AY-lee-ans), evolved into strangely shaped, shell-crunching fish called chimaeras (kie-MARE-uhs), or ratfish, which also exist today.

Over time, sharks have been able to adapt to changing ocean conditions and have become the top predators in the seas. Sharks are one of the greatest success stories of life on Earth.

A shark's vision is excellent—most sharks can see color and in extremely low light conditions.

Sharks' noses are super-sensitive. They can track a scent in the water from miles away.

Sharks have multiple rows of teeth that are replaced constantly throughout its life. That way, their teeth are always nice and sharp.

A shark's jaws are not attached directly to its skull. Instead, a network of tendons and muscles anchor the jaws and enable a shark to open its mouth extra-wide. Some sharks can actually slide their jaws forward for a more effective bite.

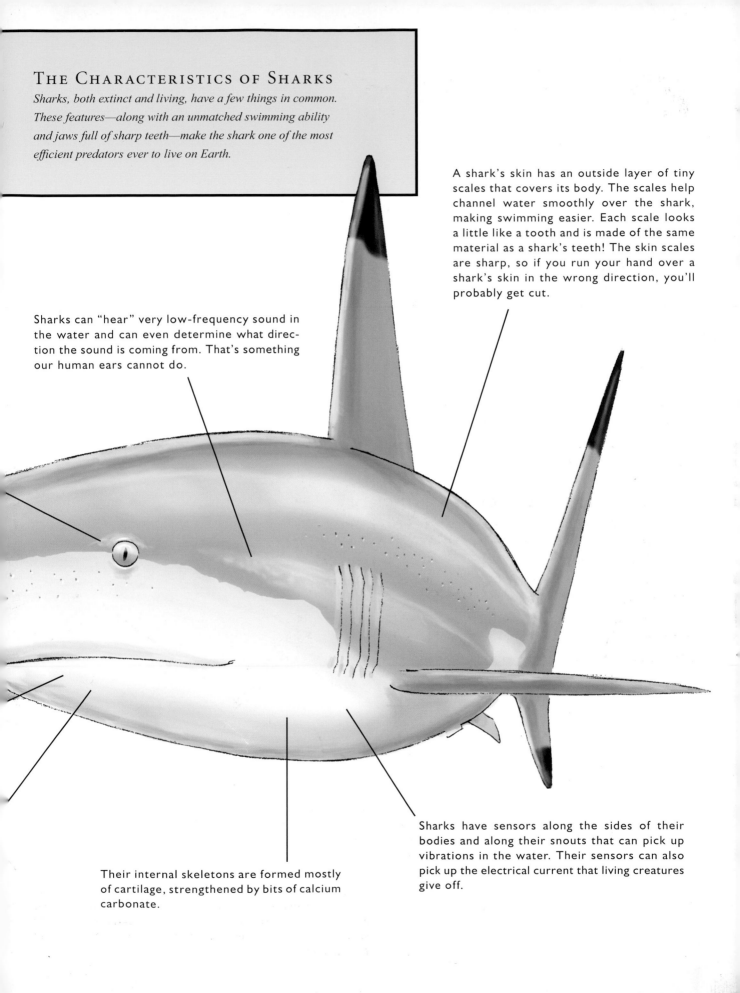

THE CHARACTERISTICS OF SHARKS

Sharks, both extinct and living, have a few things in common. These features—along with an unmatched swimming ability and jaws full of sharp teeth—make the shark one of the most efficient predators ever to live on Earth.

A shark's skin has an outside layer of tiny scales that covers its body. The scales help channel water smoothly over the shark, making swimming easier. Each scale looks a little like a tooth and is made of the same material as a shark's teeth! The skin scales are sharp, so if you run your hand over a shark's skin in the wrong direction, you'll probably get cut.

Sharks can "hear" very low-frequency sound in the water and can even determine what direction the sound is coming from. That's something our human ears cannot do.

Sharks have sensors along the sides of their bodies and along their snouts that can pick up vibrations in the water. Their sensors can also pick up the electrical current that living creatures give off.

Their internal skeletons are formed mostly of cartilage, strengthened by bits of calcium carbonate.

Paleozoic Sharks and Their Relatives
—A New Kind of Fish

IMAGINE: OVER 400 MILLION years ago, in the dark, cold waters of what is now New Brunswick, Canada, the carcass of a dead ammonite sits on the ocean bottom. It is attracting scavengers and other creatures looking for a free meal. Trilobites of all different sizes have discovered the carcass and crawl over to feed. Primitive armored fish swim clumsily by to investigate as more streamlined jawless fish wriggle through the cold water to take advantage of an easy lunch.

Suddenly, a dark shape flashes into the middle of the feast. It gulps down one of the small fish nibbling at the ammonite. Another creature zooms in and tears a chunk from the ammonite's body. Several similar shapes circle the carcass now. One at a time, they dash in and bite at the carcass or devour one of the small creatures feeding on it. These swift hunters are among the first sharks on Earth.

THIS PALEOZOIC FEEDING FRENZY might have taken place long before dinosaurs lived on this planet. There was life on land— including insects, amphibians, and later, reptiles. But fossils found around the world show that most Paleozoic life was concentrated in the oceans, rivers, lakes, and swamps.

The sharks and other chondrichthyans of the Paleozoic era include: *Cladoselache, Stethacanthus, Doliodus, Pucapampella* (an ancient chondrichthyan that might have been a shark), *Orthacanthus, Belantsea* (not a shark, but a holocephalian), *Falcatus, Promexyele* (not a shark, but a relative), and the strange *Edestus* and *Helicoprion.*

STETHACANTHUS

(STETH-UH-CANTH-US) • *375 million years ago*

STETHACANTHUS LIVED AT THE SAME TIME AS *Cladoselache*. One of the oddest-looking sharks, it was about 4 feet long. Its head and strangely shaped dorsal fin were decorated with small tooth-like spikes. Though paleontologists aren't sure what the fin and spikes were for, they might have been a threat display, making this small shark appear more fierce and dangerous than it actually was. *Stethacanthus* might also have used its fin and spikes to signal other *Stethacánthus*.

stethacanthus

dunkleosteus

CLADOSELACHE

(KLAD-OH-SELL-uh-KEE) • *375 million years ago*

Cladoselache, a 6-foot-long shark, first appeared near the very beginning of the Paleozoic era. *Cladoselache* was slender, with large fins and a powerful tail that helped it evade the giant armor-headed predatory fish *Dunkleosteus* (dunk-ull-OSS-tee-us).

Cladoselache's jaws were full of sharp teeth, but they weren't built for ripping the flesh of its prey. Instead, *Cladoselache* grabbed onto its prey, and then, tail-first, swallowed it whole.

Today, many modern fish swallow their prey headfirst to avoid the spines and barbs that many fish now have.

cladoselache

stethacanthus

great white shark

diver

cladoselache

SYMMORIUM

Symmorium *was a shark that lived at the same time and in the same areas as* Stethacanthus. *Both sharks were the same size and shape, but* Symmorium *did not have the odd fin and spikes on its body. Since no female* Stethacanthus *fossils with the strange fin and spikes have been found, some scientists think that* Symmorium *and* Stethacanthus *may have been different forms of the same shark—*Symmorium *the female, and* Stethacanthus *the male.*

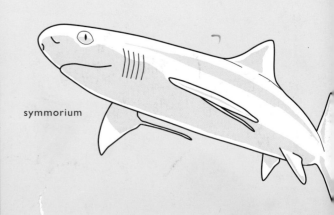

symmorium

DOLIODUS

(DOE-LEE-OH-DUS) • *360 million years ago*

DOLIODUS WAS A 30-INCH-LONG SHARK that lived during a part of the Paleozoic era scientists call the Age of Fishes in the part of the world now known as New Brunswick, Canada. A fossil of this shark is the most complete shark fossil from this time period that has been discovered so far. The fossil shark was found with its head, fins, tail—even its braincase—joined together as they would have been when the shark was alive.

Little *Doliodus* would have been no match for the large predatory fish that prowled the Paleozoic seas, but it did have some protection—spines that grew from its pectoral fins. The spines wouldn't have kept *Doliodus* completely safe, but one jab might have been enough to surprise a predator, buying enough time for *Doliodus* to escape.

Doliodus also had many rows of teeth in its upper and lower jaws, as sharks do today.

doliodus

PUCAPAMPELLA

(POOK-UH-PAM-PELL-UH) • *360 million years ago*

PUCAPAMPELLA WAS ANOTHER early chondrichthyan. Paleontologists believe it, like *Doliodus*, lived about 360 million years ago. Since very little fossil material has been found that belongs to *Pucapampella,* scientists aren't sure what it looked like, but from what they have pieced together, it seems that *Pucapampella* lived in an area of the world where the oceans were cold.

doliodus

pucapampella

great white shark

diver

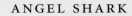

pucapampella

ANGEL SHARK

Doliodus might have looked like today's angel shark. The angel shark looks like a ray, but it is not. It has pectoral fins that help it glide along the ocean bottom. Its gills start on its underside and wrap around its sides, unlike a ray's gills which are only located on its underside.

The angel shark is an effective predator. Its mouth is full of shark teeth that are perfect for grabbing slippery fish. It lies on the sandy ocean bottom and launches itself at any prey that swims closely enough to be sucked into its mouth.

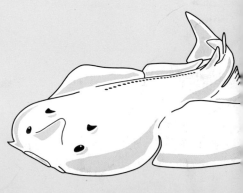

angel shark

ORTHACANTHUS

(OR-THUH-CAN-THUSS) • *360 million years ago*

ORTHACANTHUS HUNTED IN FRESHWATER lagoons about 360 million years ago. It was a member of the earliest group of sharks to live in freshwater. The group is called xenacanths (ZEE-nuh-canths), which means "strange spine," and the first xenacanths had a long spine, or spike, that grew from the back of its skull. *Orthacanthus* developed an eel-like shape, with a long fin running down its back. *Orthacanthus* was 10 feet long and had a massive set of powerful jaws, with double-fanged teeth in its wide mouth—perfect for catching the slippery fish and amphibians that swam through the muddy waters of what is now Europe and North America.

orthacanthus

orthacanthus

great white shark

diver

FRESHWATER SHARKS

*Today, not all sharks live in saltwater oceans.
The bull shark lives both in salt water and freshwater. This is amazing, since an animal used to
living in salty seawater should die in freshwater,
which has a very low salt content. But a bull
shark can conserve the salt in its body tissues
when it is living in freshwater, allowing it to survive in either environment.*

bull shark

BELANTSEA

(BELL-ANT-SEE-UH) • *350 million years ago*

BELANTSEA WAS NOT A SHARK. It was a shark relative that belonged to the holocephalian group and had a very different form. Instead of being sleek and streamlined, it was lumpy with small fins. *Belantsea*'s odd shape may have enabled it to swim through the giant sponges that grew in its habitat. Ducking into a maze of branching, colorful shapes would have been a good way for *Belantsea* to stay safe from predators.

Belantsea might even have had coloring that helped it blend in to the surrounding sponges, making it even harder for predators to attack this slow-swimming fish.

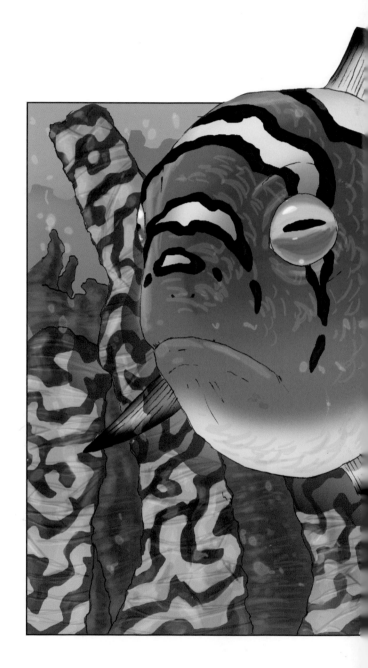

belantsea

great white shark

diver

belantsea

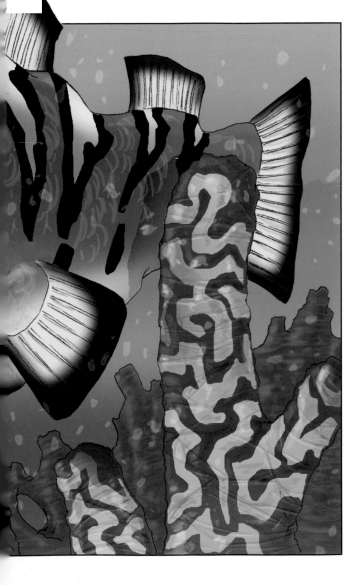

SYMBIOTIC RELATIONSHIPS

A symbiotic relationship is a relationship between two different kinds of animals or plants that help each other. For example, the present-day clown fish spends its life among the deadly stinging tentacles of sea anemones. Amazingly, the anemone does not sting the clown fish. In fact, it provides a safe place for the clown fish to live. In turn, the clown fish helps to clean the anemone and it may even chase away the anemone's predators. The ancient Belantsea *might have had a symbiotic relationship with the corals, sponges, or other creatures populating the oceans of 350 million years ago.* Belantsea *might have fed on small predators that threatened ancient corals or sponges, and in return, it might have enjoyed the safety of hiding among the sponge beds or coral reefs of the Paleozoic era.*

clown fish
with an anemone

FALCATUS

(FAL-KATE-US) • *320 million years ago*

TWELVE-INCH-LONG FALCATUS had large eyes that helped it hunt the small shrimp it ate. Male *Falcatus* had a strange hook-shaped spine growing over the front of their heads. *Falcatus* was a close relative of *Stethacanthus,* the spiky-finned shark from earlier in the Paleozoic era. The use of the spine is not known, but it might have been a signal to warn other male *Falcatus* away or to attract female *Falcatus.*

Fossils of *Falcatus* have been found together, possibly indicating that this shark might have traveled in schools.

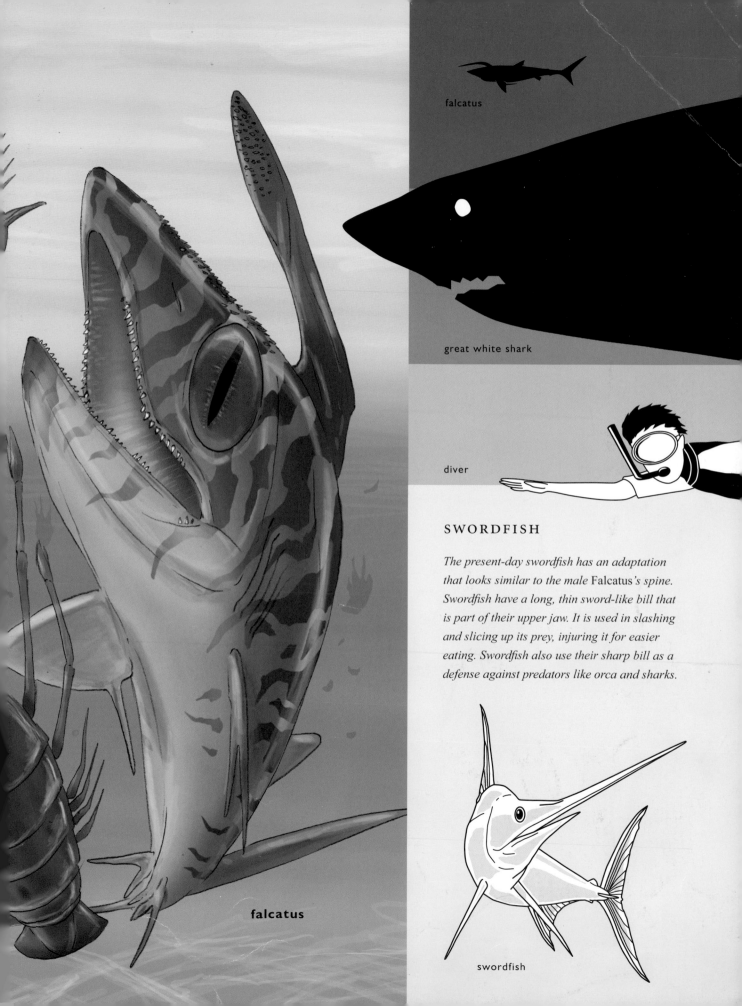

falcatus

great white shark

diver

SWORDFISH

The present-day swordfish has an adaptation that looks similar to the male Falcatus's spine. Swordfish have a long, thin sword-like bill that is part of their upper jaw. It is used in slashing and slicing up its prey, injuring it for easier eating. Swordfish also use their sharp bill as a defense against predators like orca and sharks.

falcatus

swordfish

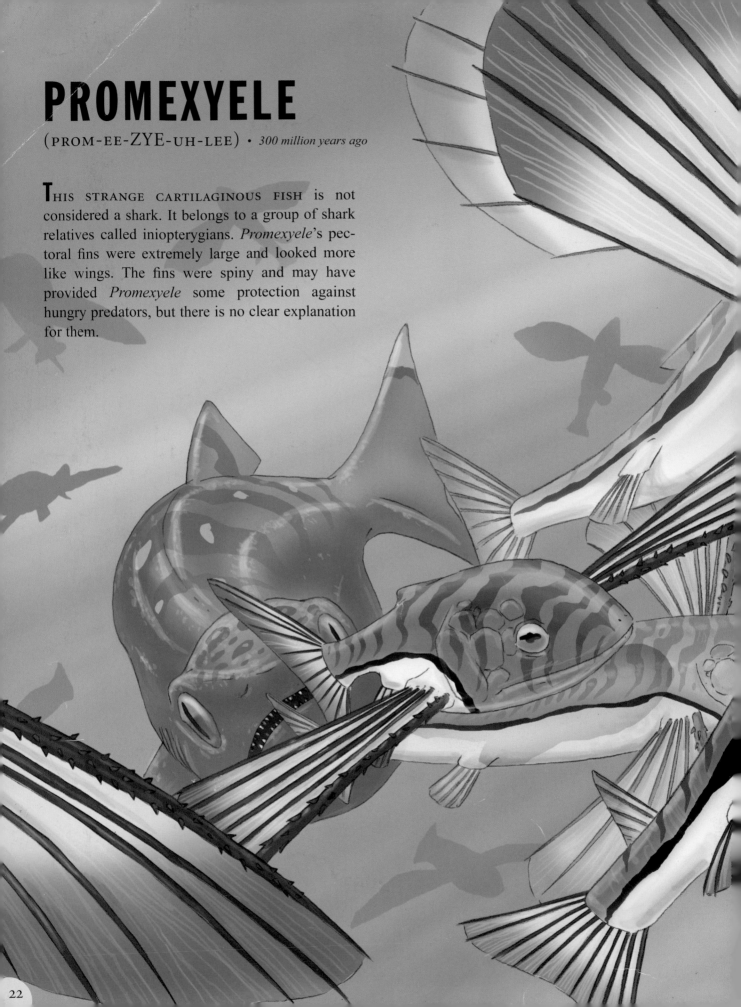

PROMEXYELE

(PROM-EE-ZYE-UH-LEE) • *300 million years ago*

THIS STRANGE CARTILAGINOUS FISH is not considered a shark. It belongs to a group of shark relatives called iniopterygians. *Promexyele*'s pectoral fins were extremely large and looked more like wings. The fins were spiny and may have provided *Promexyele* some protection against hungry predators, but there is no clear explanation for them.

promexyele

promexyele

great white shark

diver

LIONFISH

A modern-day fish that uses spines for defense is the lionfish. Lionfish have many spines on their bodies that can be used to slice any intruder that gets too close. The spines are also venomous and are enough to discourage even the most determined predator.

lionfish

EDESTUS

(EE-DEST-us) • *300 million years ago*

Edestus was one of the most fearsome predators of its time. At 20 feet long, it was about the size of a present-day great white shark.

Edestus had one of the strangest jaws ever. Like many other sharks, *Edestus* continually grew new teeth to replace old or damaged ones. However, fossil evidence indicates that *Edestus* had a middle row of teeth that grew out of its lower jaw. *Edestus*'s strange row of extended teeth might have made it easier for it to injure or disable its prey before devouring it.

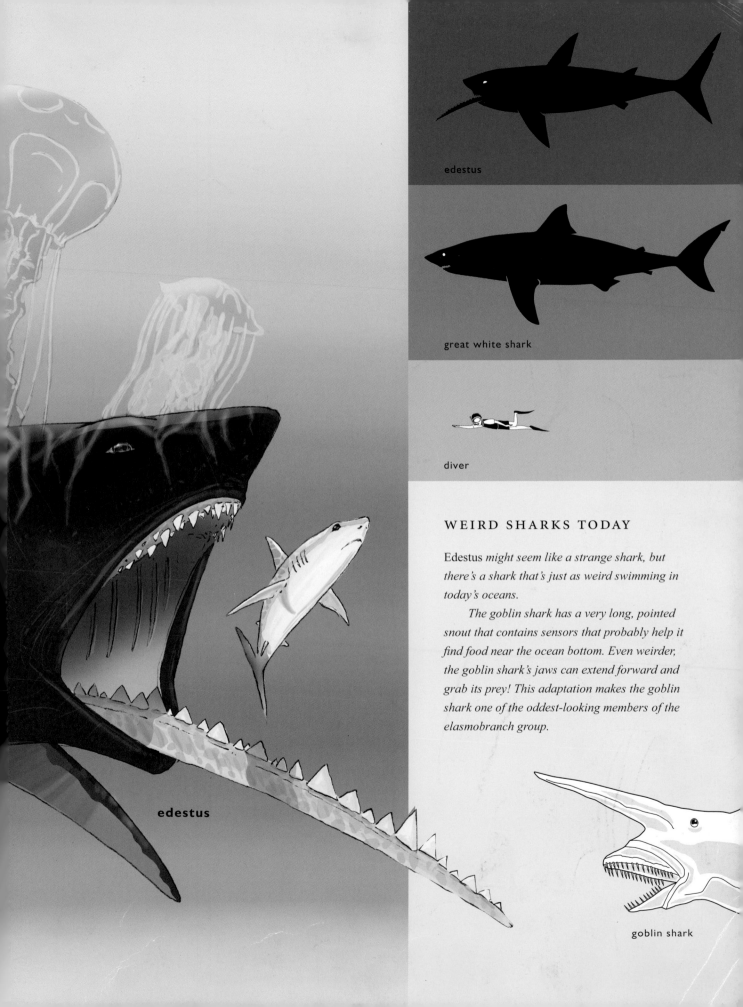

edestus

great white shark

diver

edestus

WEIRD SHARKS TODAY

Edestus *might seem like a strange shark, but there's a shark that's just as weird swimming in today's oceans.*

The goblin shark has a very long, pointed snout that contains sensors that probably help it find food near the ocean bottom. Even weirder, the goblin shark's jaws can extend forward and grab its prey! This adaptation makes the goblin shark one of the oddest-looking members of the elasmobranch group.

goblin shark

HELICOPRION

(HEEL-IK-KOE-PRY-ON) · *250 million years ago*

Edestus wasn't the only ancient shark with a bizarre jaw. Fossil evidence suggests that *Helicoprion* had hundreds of teeth tightly packed into a compact spiral that looked like a 10-inch buzz-saw blade! *Helicoprion* lived about 250 million years ago, and very little fossil evidence of these creatures has been found, but what has been uncovered mystifies paleontologists.

Helicoprion might have used its buzz-saw jaw to injure or kill as it swam swiftly through a school of squid or other prey, similar to the way modern-day sawfish use their toothy snouts.

helicoprion

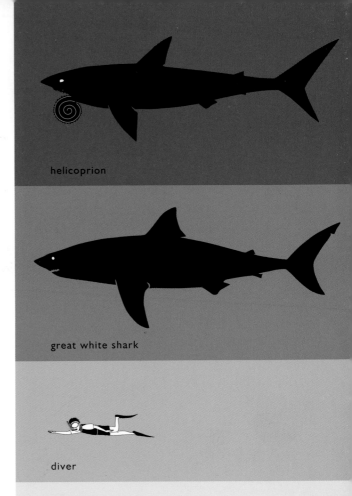

helicoprion

great white shark

diver

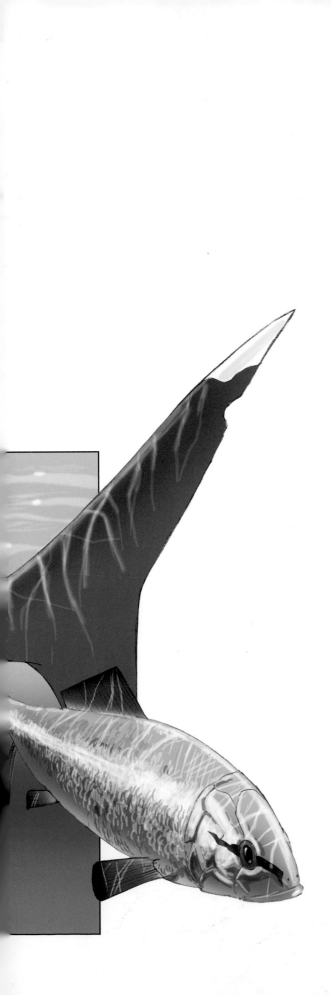

HELICOPRION'S MYSTERIOUS BUZZ-SAW JAW

When fossils of Helicoprion's buzz-saw-like jaw were first found, scientists couldn't figure out where on the shark's body they belonged. Did they go on the shark's back in front of its dorsal fin, in the shark's upper jaw, or coiled up as a whip-like weapon that hung from its lower jaw? Scientists still aren't sure exactly how these tooth spirals fit into Helicoprion's mouth, but it is possible that they fit between the left and right sides of the lower jaw and probably hung below it. As new teeth grew in Helicoprion's jaw, older teeth were pushed out and forward, eventually coiling up into a tightly packed mass of shark teeth.

Mesozoic Sharks and Their Relatives
—Reptilian Competition

IMAGINE: IT'S SUMMERTIME about 200 million years ago. A pack of 12-foot-long *Hybodus* sharks enter the warm waters near the area now known as Europe. They're following a school of silver-scaled fish.

As they swim, the sharks pick up vibrations of several approaching creatures. The sharks spread out warily; they can tell that the creatures are larger than they are. Suddenly, three 15-foot-long creatures with long writhing necks and jaws full of needle-sharp teeth slash through the group of the fish. Very few of the fish get away in time.

The creatures are new to these waters. They are called *Macroplata* and they are fish-eaters. Sharks are fish.

Two of the *Macroplata* veer suddenly and attack one of the *Hybodus*. Within seconds, the blood in the water attracts other scavengers. *Hybodus* is no longer the top predator in this part of the ocean.

hybodus

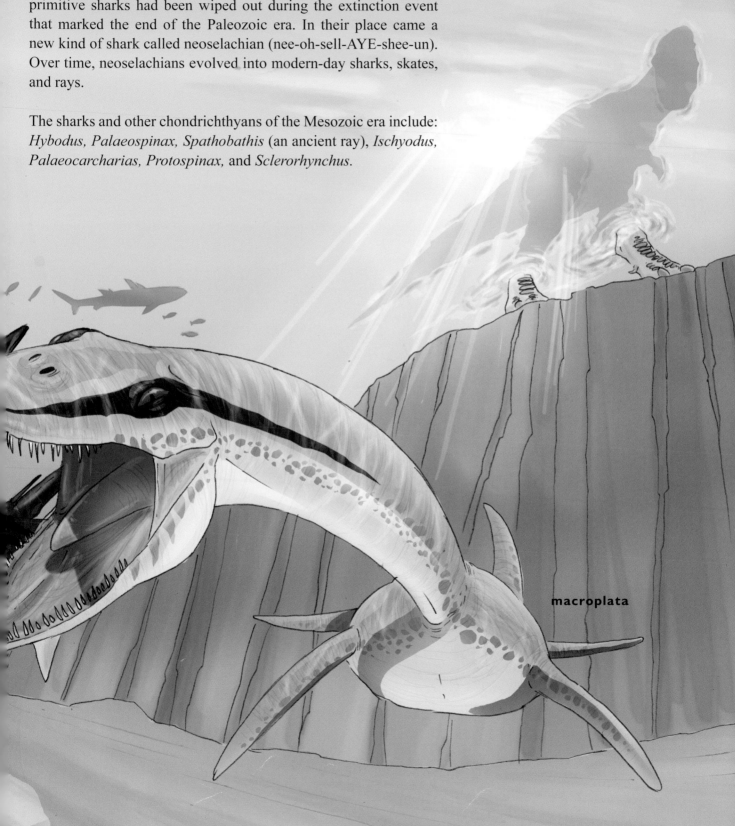

DURING THE MESOZOIC ERA, new kinds of aquatic reptiles developed. They were very effective predators and hunted in the seas for the next 150 million years.

Sharks and their relatives were there, too. Most of the more primitive sharks had been wiped out during the extinction event that marked the end of the Paleozoic era. In their place came a new kind of shark called neoselachian (nee-oh-sell-AYE-shee-un). Over time, neoselachians evolved into modern-day sharks, skates, and rays.

The sharks and other chondrichthyans of the Mesozoic era include: *Hybodus, Palaeospinax, Spathobathis* (an ancient ray), *Ischyodus, Palaeocarcharias, Protospinax,* and *Sclerorhynchus.*

macroplata

HYBODUS

(HI-BOE-DUS) · *180 million years ago*

DURING THE MESOZOIC ERA, *Hybodus* became one of the most numerous sharks in the world's oceans. But scientists believe that *Hybodus* didn't stop there. *Hybodus* were also able to survive in freshwater, much like today's bull shark.

Hybodus grew to about 12 feet long with a shape like that of today's great white shark, and was probably just as effective at catching prey. *Hybodus* had spines poking from its dorsal fins and the sides of its head. A defense against predators or a way to spot another *Hybodus*? Scientists aren't sure.

hybodus

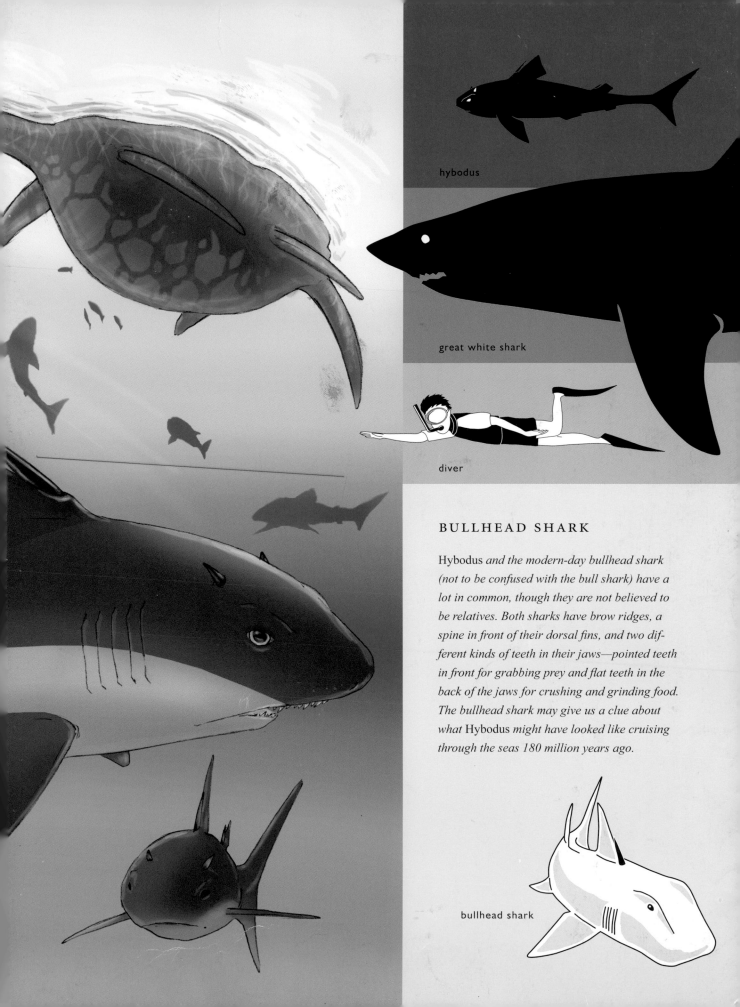

hybodus

great white shark

diver

BULLHEAD SHARK

Hybodus *and the modern-day bullhead shark (not to be confused with the bull shark) have a lot in common, though they are not believed to be relatives. Both sharks have brow ridges, a spine in front of their dorsal fins, and two different kinds of teeth in their jaws—pointed teeth in front for grabbing prey and flat teeth in the back of the jaws for crushing and grinding food. The bullhead shark may give us a clue about what* Hybodus *might have looked like cruising through the seas 180 million years ago.*

bullhead shark

PALAEOSPINAX

(PALE-EE-OH-SPINE-AX) · *180 million years ago*

PALAEOSPINAX'S SLIM 3-FOOT-LONG BODY and large pectoral fins made it a swift, maneuverable hunter. Its speed also helped it escape from hungry predators. Very little fossil evidence of *Palaeospinax* has been discovered, so paleontologists aren't sure how to classify this little shark. They think *Palaeospinax* is part of the neoselachian group. Neoselachians (which means "new sharks") first appeared in the Paleozoic era.

palaeospinax

palaeospinax

great white shark

diver

NEOSELACHIAN SHARKS

*During the Mesozoic era, the seas were full
of giant schools of bony fish, a bountiful food
source for any predator fast enough to catch
them. To eat these bony fish, sharks in the
neoselachian group became faster, more skillful
swimmers, and developed jaws that were more
flexible than those of earlier sharks. These
advantages enabled neoselachians to flourish,
but they had fierce competition from ocean-
swimming reptiles.*

SPATHOBATHIS

(SPATH-OH-BATH-ISS) · *160 million years ago*

Spathobathis is one of the earliest rays. Its body was basically shark-like, but over time *Spathobathis* evolved some special adaptations that helped it survive on the sea bottom. It had a long snout, which may have helped it probe the sand for food. Its mouth—full of flat, broad teeth—was located under its body, perfect for scooping up shellfish. *Spathobathis* had broad, wing-like pectoral fins that were great for gliding over the ocean floor, and with its eyes on top of its head, it could easily spot danger from above. *Spathobathis* was similar to the banjo ray, a fish that lives on the bottom of today's oceans.

spathobathis

ISCHYODUS

(IS-KEE-OH-DUS) · *150 million years ago*

ISCHYODUS WAS NOT A SHARK, but a 5-foot-long member of the holocephalian group of cartilaginous fish. *Ischyodus*'s strong jaws and large tooth plates made it a fearsome predator. It had a long ribbon-like tail, a spine in front of its dorsal fin—which in modern species of cartilaginous fish can be poisonous—and the characteristic holocephalian snout. *Ischyodus* might have been strange looking, but it was part of a group of creatures that has survived for hundreds of millions of years!

spathobathis

ischyodus

great white shark

diver

ischyodus

RAYS

Rays like Spathobathis *are relatives of sharks. Like sharks, rays do not have skeletons made of bone but of cartilage. Rays have flattened bodies, and many live on the ocean bottom, munching on shellfish and small creatures. In our oceans today, there are many kinds of rays. Some rays swim together in giant schools, sometimes numbering in the thousands.*

The largest ray is the manta, whose giant, flattened body can be up to 22 feet across. It glides gracefully through the ocean, scooping microscopic plankton and small fish into its mouth with the small fins that extend forward from its head.

manta ray

PALAEOCARCHARIAS

(PALE-EE-OH-CAR-CARE-EE-US) · *150 million years ago*

PALAEOCARCHARIAS WAS A MEMBER of the line of sharks that led to present-day bull sharks and hammerhead sharks. *Palaeocarcharias* had a powerful, sleek body and large pectoral fins that might have given it good directional control while chasing its prey.

palaeocarcharias

PROTOSPINAX

(PRO-TOE-SPINE-AX) • *150 million years ago*

P ROTOSPINAX WAS RELATED to the modern-day angel shark or saw shark. Its body was very stream-lined—like the bodies of our present-day sharks—but its fins were broad and flat, like a ray's. Some scientists believe sharks and rays belong to separate groups, while others think *Protospinax* is a "missing link" between the two. Until more about this shark is discovered, no one can say which view is correct.

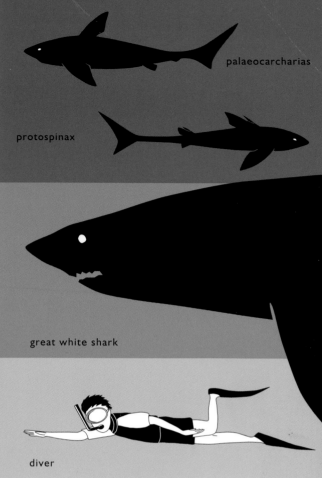

palaeocarcharias

protospinax

great white shark

diver

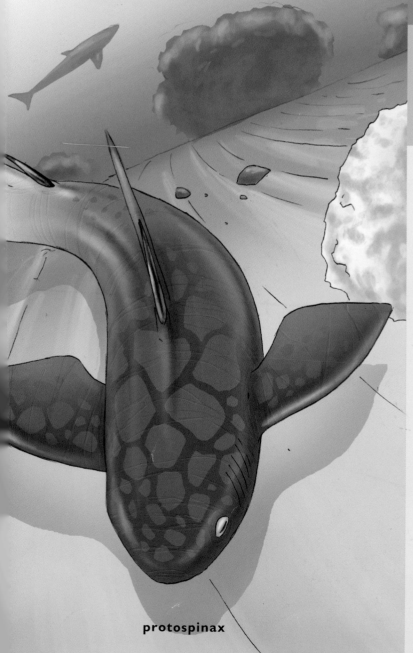

protospinax

HAMMERHEAD SHARKS

The hammerhead shark is one of the most instantly recognizable sharks in the ocean today. Its head resembles a hammer. This wide flat head shape is a very useful adaptation for a shark that searches the ocean bottom for some of its food! The hammerhead's head acts like a wing, helping it glide through the water. Having wide-set eyes helps the hammerhead see a wider area of the ocean, giving it a better chance to spot food. Its head is also full of sensors that help it find prey that's buried in the sand.

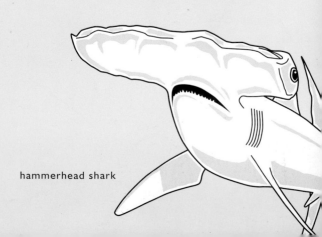

hammerhead shark

SCLERORHYNCHUS

(SKLARE-OH-RINK-USS) • *80 million years ago*

Sclerorhynchus looked remarkably like our modern-day sawfish. It had large fins for gliding just above the seafloor to look for food. It had a flat body and a long snout studded with sharp tooth-like scales. *Sclerorhynchus* might have used its snout to slice up its prey and make it easier to swallow. Present-day sawfish use their saw-like snouts in this way. The teeth inside *Sclerorhynchus*'s mouth were very small.

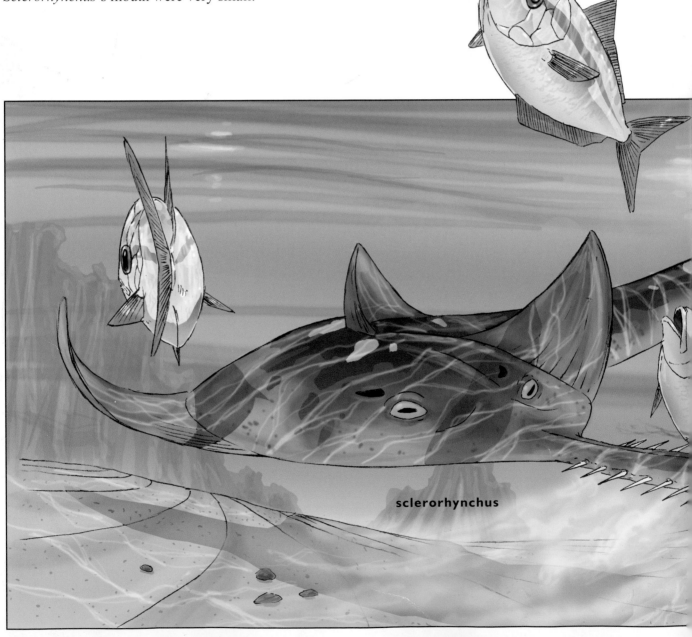

sclerorhynchus

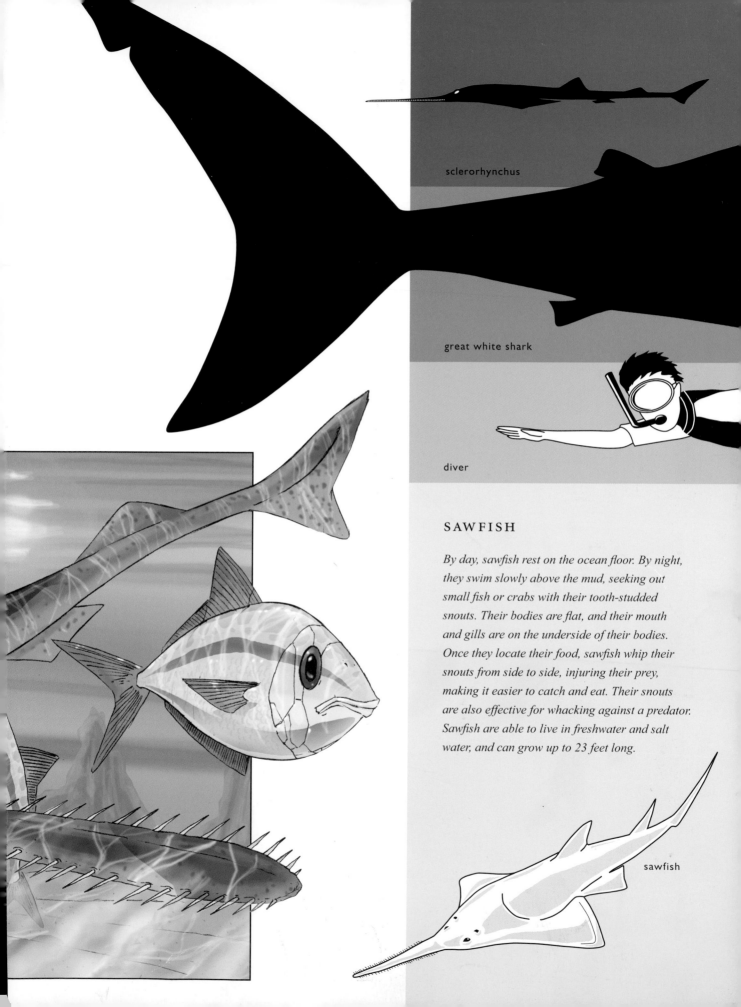

sclerorhynchus

great white shark

diver

SAWFISH

By day, sawfish rest on the ocean floor. By night, they swim slowly above the mud, seeking out small fish or crabs with their tooth-studded snouts. Their bodies are flat, and their mouth and gills are on the underside of their bodies. Once they locate their food, sawfish whip their snouts from side to side, injuring their prey, making it easier to catch and eat. Their snouts are also effective for whacking against a predator. Sawfish are able to live in freshwater and salt water, and can grow up to 23 feet long.

sawfish

Cenozoic Shark
—Swimming Nightmare

IMAGINE: A POD OF WHALES cruises through the ocean. They stay close to the warmer surface waters, because that is where the little creatures they feed on live. There are about 15 whales in the pod, mostly adults, with the young ones toward the middle for safety. They are migrating toward their summer waters, taking their time, clicking and whistling to one another.

A school of sharks follows the pod closely. The whales aren't worried. The sharks won't attack healthy whales; they are too much trouble. Suddenly, the sharks scatter as something rushes up from the ocean depths. The whales draw close together for protection, but it is no use.

A huge creature resembling a great white shark in shape, but much larger, rams into the pod. At 50 feet long, it is almost four times the length of the adult whales, and it weighs close to 100,000 pounds. On its first pass, it devours two of the young whales whole. When the monster turns, it opens its jaws to reveal triangular, razor-edged teeth that seem to reach out of its mouth. It closes on a whale, slicing it in half and swallowing its head without slowing down.

This scene might have taken place 25 million years ago, during the Miocene period. The huge shark was *Carcharodon megalodon,* possibly the largest predatory shark that ever lived, and the most dangerous creature in the Cenozoic seas.

CARCHARODON MEGALODON

(CAR-CAR-OH-DON MEG-UH-LOW-DON) • *25 million years ago*

MEGALODON WAS VERY SIMILAR to today's great white shark—except in size. The great white can grow to about 25 feet long and weigh about 2 tons (4,000 pounds). But scientists believe megalodon grew up to 50 feet long and might have weighed close to 50 tons!

Megalodon ate anything it wanted. Its huge and powerful jaws were packed with 6-inch-tall, razor-edged, triangular teeth that sliced through its prey. Megalodon probably hunted the biggest fish and whales that swam the oceans of the Cenozoic era.

megalodon

great white shark

diver

megalodon

MEGALODON RECONSTRUCTION

Several paleontologists are still figuring out exactly what the megalodon looked like. Typically, sharks don't fossilize well, since their skeletons are mostly cartilage and not bone. Most megalodon fossils found are of its giant teeth, although a few vertebrae have also been recovered. Since the megalodon's teeth closely resemble those of the present-day great white shark, scientists use the great white's body as a starting point. However, to recreate the megalodon, scientists must make the body stouter and heavier, with more massive jaws and teeth.

Sharks Today

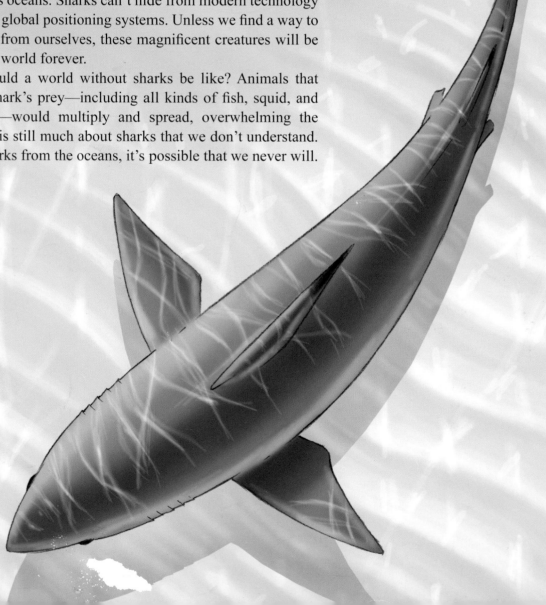

SHARKS HAVE SURVIVED for over 400 million years, weathering drastic climate changes, shifting continents, competition from marine reptiles, and several devastating extinctions that wiped out untold numbers of animals and plants. They are a true evolutionary success.

However, today's sharks are once again in danger of extinction. For the first time in their long history, they are not threatened by meteor impact, a change in Earth's weather patterns, or any other natural cause.

Sharks are threatened by us. Humans hunt sharks for food and sport in today's oceans. Sharks can't hide from modern technology like sonar, and global positioning systems. Unless we find a way to protect sharks from ourselves, these magnificent creatures will be gone from our world forever.

What would a world without sharks be like? Animals that are now the shark's prey—including all kinds of fish, squid, and sea mammals—would multiply and spread, overwhelming the oceans. There is still much about sharks that we don't understand. If we wipe sharks from the oceans, it's possible that we never will.

Glossary

AMMONITE (AM-OH-NITE):
ancient shelled sea creatures that were related to today's octopus.

CARTILAGE (KART-IH-LUJ):
a flexible material that some fish have instead of bone.

CHONDRICHTHYANS (KON-DRIK-THEE-ANS):
fish with skeletons made of cartilage, which includes elasmobranchs and holocephalians, as well as their extinct common ancestors.

ELASMOBRANCHS (EE-LAZ-MOE-BRANKS):
one of two groups of fish that over millions of years evolved into modern sharks and rays, as well as their extinct relatives.

ERA (EER-AH):
a period of time that scientists use to divide Earth's history.

EVOLUTION (EE-VOE-LOO-SHUN):
a scientific idea, or theory, that describes how a living thing inherits traits or characteristics from its parents. These changes are passed from parents to offspring through genes, the blueprints contained in every living thing's cells. Genes describe how an animal, or plant, or you *should be made.*

EXTINCT (EX-TINKT):
a term used to describe an organism that has totally died out, so that there are none left living anywhere on Earth.

FOSSIL (FOSS-IL):
a preserved trace, like a bone or footprint, left by an animal that has died.

HOLOCEPHALIANS (HOL-OH-SEFF-ALE-EE-ANS):
one of two groups of ancient chondrichthyan fish that evolved into strangely shaped, shell-crunching modern fish called chimaeras, or ratfish.

INIOPTERYGIAN (IN-EE-OP-TER-IJ-EE-AN):
a group of ancient chondrichthyan fish that may have been closely related to holocephalians.

NEOSELACHIAN (NEE-OH-SELL-AYE-SHEE-UN):
the family of sharks that appeared in the Mesozoic era that eventually evolved into present-day sharks and rays.

PECTORAL FIN (PEK-TOR-AL FIN):
a fin located on either side of a fish's body, near its head, which helps it steer through the water.

RECONSTRUCTION (RE-KON-STRUK-SHUN):
to use fossil evidence to show what an extinct creature may have been like by making a sculpture or drawing of it.

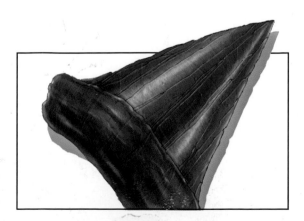

Further Reading

FOR YOUNGER READERS:

JURASSIC SHARK
by Deborah Diffily
illustrated by Karen Carr
HarperCollins, 2004
About the life of an individual *Hybodus* shark.

GIANT SHARK: MEGALODON,
PREHISTORIC SUPER PREDATOR
by Caroline Arnold
illustrated by Laurie Caple
Clarion Books, 2000
Great information and illustrations about what
could have been the most fearsome shark ever.

THE TRUTH ABOUT GREAT WHITE
SHARKS
by Mary Cerullo
photographs by Jeffrey L. Rotman
illustrations by Michael Wertz
Chronicle Books, 2000
A fun book all about everyone's favorite ocean
predator.

FOR OLDER READERS AND ADULTS:

SHARKS
by Doug Perrine
Voyageur Press, 2002
An informative general book about present-day
sharks.

PLANET OCEAN: A STORY OF LIFE,
THE SEA, AND DANCING TO THE
FOSSIL RECORD
by Brad Matsen
illustrated by Ray Troll
Ten Speed Press, 1994
A fun-to-read book relating the author's and
illustrator's journey to find out about life's
beginnings in the seas.

DISCOVERING FOSSIL FISHES
by Dr. John G. Maisey
illustrations by David Miller and Ivy Rutzky
photographs by Craig Chesek and Dennis Finnin
Westview Press, 2000
A definitive and in-depth look at ancient fish
packed with factual information, with wonderful
illustrations and photos.